MARGARET MILLER

GUESS WHO?

GREENWILLOW BOOKS, NEW YORK

The generous and good-natured cooperation of the many children and grown-ups in *Guess Who?* made this project a delight. Thank you all: AAA Imported Motors; Olga Allen; the Bank Street School for Children; Miranda Berman; Annie Bernard; Scott Blumenthal; Evelyn Casella; Victor V. Delgado; Heidi P. Higgins; Hot & Crusty; Paul Howard; Benjamin Jakubowski; Charlie Jurgens; Mark Kaplan; Peter Kelly; Michael Lee; Charles Long; Carlos Lucero; John G. Mattarazzo; Grayson Means; Barbara Miller; Jaclyn, Jacob, and Cathy Miller; Susie Moser; the New York Yankees; Leonie Norton; Keith Osterbrink; Daniela Palma; Dina G. Pascasio, D.M.D.; Pet Shop Ltd.; Kyle Rappaport; Alexandra Rodriguez; Kim Rosenthal, D.V.M.; Lewie Scott; Michael Suhu; the U.S. Marine Corps Band; Ottmar Weber; and Sue Burdick Young.

The full-color photographs were reproduced from 35-mm Kodachrome 25 slides. The text type is Avant Garde.

LIBRARY OF CONGRESS CATALOGING-IN-PUBLICATION DATA
Miller, Margaret (date)
Guess who? / by Margaret Miller.
     p.   cm.
Summary: A child is asked who delivers the mail, gives haircuts, flies an airplane, and performs other important tasks. Each question has several different answers from which to choose.
ISBN 0-688-12783-5 (trade).   ISBN 0-688-12784-3 (lib. bdg.)
(1. Occupations—Fiction.   2. Literary recreations.)   I. Title.
PZ7.M628Gu   1994   (E)—dc20   93-26704   CIP   AC

For Ava,

who brings out the best in my books

Who goes to school?

Seagulls?

Puppies?

Umpires?

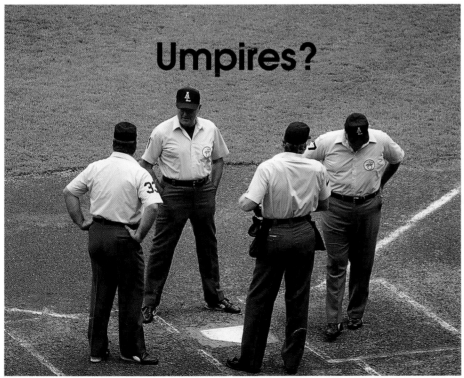

Stuffed animals?

Children!

Who cleans your teeth?

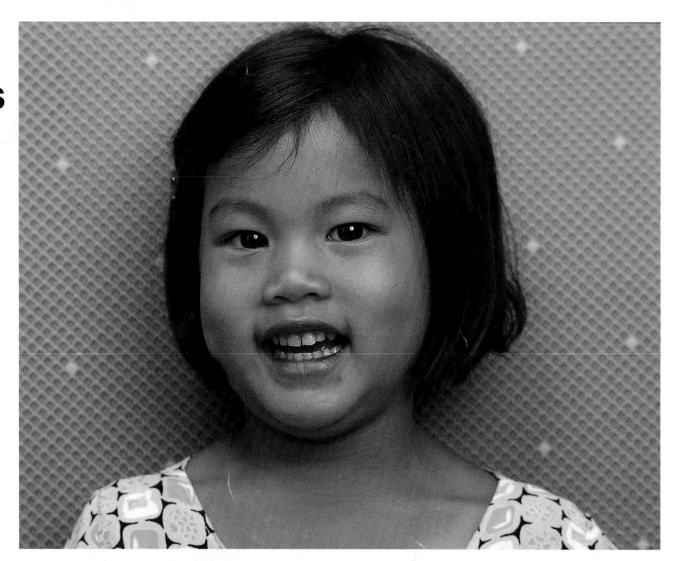

A cat?

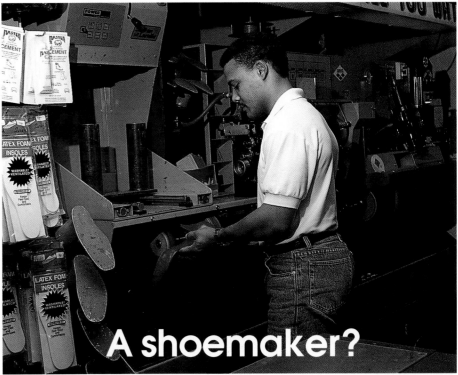

A shoemaker?

A window washer?

A rubber duckie?

A dentist!

Who cuts your hair?

A chef?

A tailor?

A gardener?

A polar bear?

A barber!

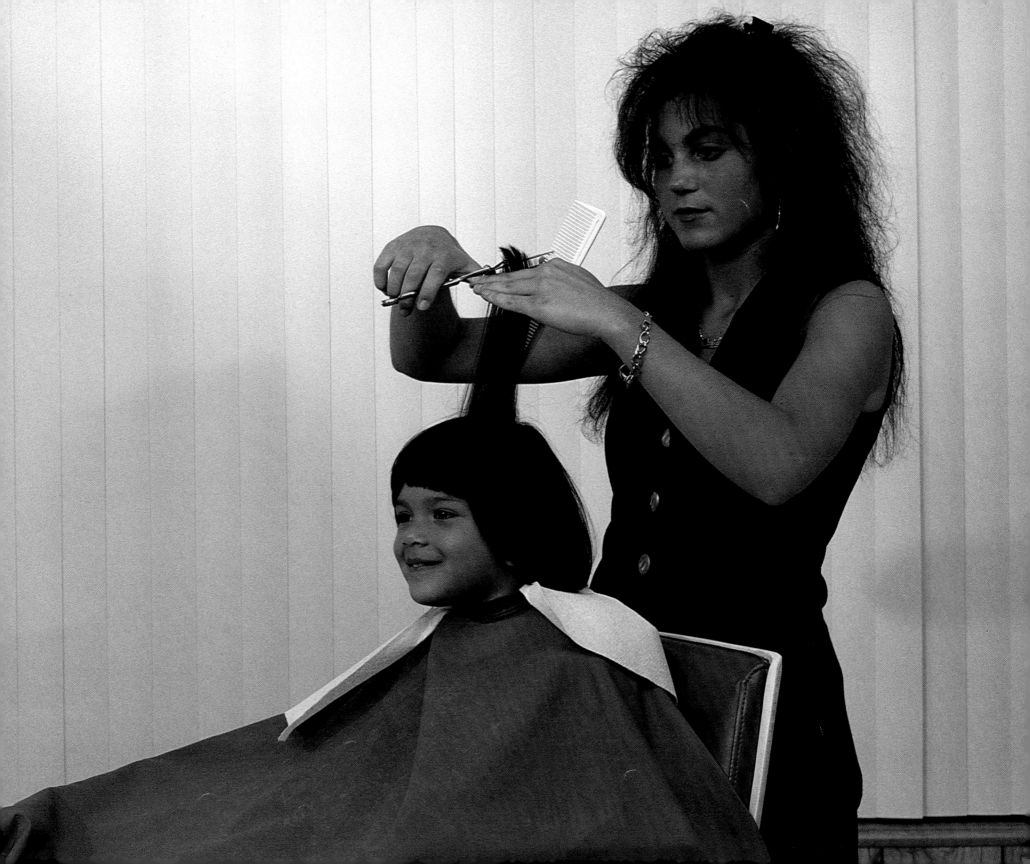

Who
wakes
you
in the
morning?

A hot-air balloon?

A puppet?

A lion?

A military band?

Your dog!

Who flies an airplane?

A bus driver?

A statue?

A turtle?

A baby?

A pilot!

Who makes your bread?

A giraffe?

A juggler?

An artist?

A potter?

A baker!

Who fixes your car?

A crab?

A plumber?

A clown?

A veterinarian?

A mechanic!

Who delivers your mail?

A magician?

A pitcher?

A police officer?

A parrot?

A letter carrier!

Who takes your picture?

A violinist?

A monkey?

A dog groomer?

A carpenter?

A photographer!

MARGARET MILLER is a freelance photographer who lives in New York City with her husband, two children, and two dogs. She traces her love of photography to her childhood. "My mother is a wonderful photographer and I grew up in a house filled with family photographs. I especially loved being with her in the darkroom. I also spent many hours looking through two very powerful books, *The Family of Man* edited by Edward Steichen, and *You Have Seen Their Faces* by Erskine Caldwell and Margaret Bourke-White. After college I worked in children's book publishing for a number of years. I had always taken photographs of my family and I was fortunate in realizing my goal of combining my two long-time interests—photography and children's books."

Margaret Miller is the author/photographer of *Whose Hat?*; *Who Uses This?*; *Whose Shoe?*; *Where Does It Go?*, a *New York Times* Best Illustrated Book of 1992; and *Can You Guess?* She is also the photographer for *Ramona: Behind the Scenes of a Television Show*; *Funny Papers*; *The President Builds a House*; *Your New Potty*; *My Puppy Is Born*; and *How You Were Born.*